This Topsy and Tim
book belongs to

_____

Topsy + Tim

have a birthday party

Jean and Gareth Adamson

Ladybird

All Ladybird books are available at most bookshops, supermarkets
and newsagents, or can be ordered direct from:
Ladybird Postal Sales PO Box 133 Paignton TQ3 2YP England
Telephone: (+44) 01803 554761 *Fax:* (+44) 01803 663394

A catalogue record for this book is available from the British Library

Published by Ladybird Books Ltd
A subsidiary of the Penguin Group
A Pearson Company

© Jean and Gareth Adamson MCMXCV
This edition MCMXCVIII

It was Topsy and Tim's birthday.
The first thing they saw when
they woke up was a pile of
birthday presents.

The postman brought them lots of
birthday cards and a package
from Granny.

'Happy birthday, twins,' he said.
'How did you know it was
our birthday?' asked Topsy.
'I guessed!' laughed the postman.

After breakfast, Topsy and Tim went into the garden to try out their new roller skates.

'Happy birthday, Topsy and Tim,'
shouted their friends over the fence.
'How did you know it was our
birthday?' asked Tim.
'Because you've invited us to your
party this afternoon, silly,'
said Stevie Dunton.

Later, Dad took them to the shops
to buy party balloons and candles
for their birthday cake.

'Happy birthday, Topsy and Tim,'
said Mrs Patel.
'How did you know it was our birthday?'
asked Topsy and Tim.
'A little bird told me,' said Mrs Patel.

When they got home, Topsy and Tim
helped to get everything ready
for their birthday party. Dad
showed them how to blow up the balloons.

Then they hung the balloons
in bright bunches round the room.

Topsy and Tim and Dad went into
the kitchen to help make the
party tea. Mummy showed Topsy
how to ice the little cakes.
Tim stuck a sweet on top of
each one.

Dad was putting sticks into the party sausages. He popped a sausage into his mouth, then gave one each to Topsy and Tim.
'Stop that,' said Mummy, 'or there won't be any left for the party.'

'Can Tim and I put the candles
on our birthday cake?' asked Topsy.
'No,' said Mummy. 'You're having
a surprise birthday cake, so
I'll put the candles on. You can
help Dad put the food on the tea table.'

Topsy and Tim enjoyed carrying the wibbly wobbly jellies.

Everything was ready for the party.
Then their friends began to arrive.
Vinda was the first, then Tony Welch.
Stevie Dunton and Andy Anderson
came together. 'Here I am,' said Kerry.
Rai was just behind.

They had all brought birthday presents
for Topsy and Tim.
'Is everyone here?' asked Mummy.
'Everyone except Josie,' said Topsy.
'We can't start without Josie,' said Tim.
'I think we'd better,' said Mummy.

First they played Musical Chairs.
Dad played the music. Each time
the music stopped, they had to
find a chair to sit on.
'I've not got a chair,' said Topsy.
'You're out, then,' said Dad.
Stevie Dunton won Musical Chairs.
Mummy gave him a prize.

Next they played Oranges and Lemons.
Mummy and Dad made the arch and
'Oranges and lemons, say the bells
of St Clement's . . .'

'Time for one more game before tea,'
said Mummy. 'We'll play Pass the Parcel.'
Just then, the doorbell rang.
It was Josie Miller.
'Hooray,' said Topsy and Tim.

Josie sat down between Topsy and
Tim and the music began. Every time
the music stopped, the one holding
the parcel had to unwrap it a bit more.
'Everybody's won something except me,'
grumbled Josie. Then she won
Pass the Parcel. 'This is a good party,'
said Josie.

'Time for the birthday tea,' said Dad.
There was plenty of food for
everyone and lots of orange
to drink.
'I *was* thirsty,' said Andy Anderson.

Mummy came in with the surprise
birthday cake. 'Ooh, it's a dinosaur!'
said the children.
The dinosaur had candles all down
its back.

All the children sang 'Happy Birthday' and Topsy and Tim blew out their birthday candles with one big puff.